I am Afraid

of the

DARK

Written and Illustrated by

DEBORAH ROWE JOHNSON

I am Afraid of the **DARK**
Sunny Me®
Deborah Rowe Johnson DESIGNS

ISBN 978-1-0980-0838-3 (paperback)
ISBN 978-1-0980-0840-6 (hardcover)
ISBN 978-1-0980-0839-0 (digital)

Christian Faith Publishing, Inc.
832 Park Avenue
Meadville, PA 16335
www.christianfaithpublishing.com

Printed in the United States of America

I am Afraid

of the

DARK

God's Reflections, Inc. ®

God is light
and in him
there is no darkness

May you experience the joy and happiness
that light, truth, and friendship can bring.

Sunshine, Sunshine...we love it!

Is this a dream?
Am I having a Nightmare?

Oh my...
It is really **DARK**!
I can't see...I can't see...
I am scared!

Help! Help!
I am really SCARED!

"I hate the **DARK**."

Hey, Bobby Lee...
Where are you?
Bobby Lee, where are you?
Can you see me?

Oh no, my best friend Bobby Lee,
the "bumble bee," can't see me...
and I can't find him.

Where is Bobby Lee?
Slip, slip, trip, fall

How can I get to the light?

Wait... I hear something!

**BZZZZZ-----BZZZZZZ---
BZZZZZZZ--BZZZZZZZ**

Oh thank goodness
I can hear the zoom of the bee.
Hee...Hee...
it has got to be Bobby Lee.

Hey, Sunny Me, I found you,
hummed Bobby Lee.

Tor-ment-ing Tornadoes

How did it get so **DARK** in here?

8

Sunny Me says, "Bobby Lee, I had a bad dream!"
I was outside in a rainstorm and
the sky was pitch black.
It was so **DARK**, and I did not
know how I got there.

I said to myself,
"Why am I all alone, standing in the
street, during a BAD STORM?"

In just a blink, I could have been struck by lightning.

Oh me...Oh my...
in the blink of an eye,

SUNNY ME...CR-INK-LED

by a **Bolt of Lightning!**

Thank you Lord for using my friend, Bobby Lee,
to wake me up from this bad dream...
I mean terri-fy-ing nightmare!

SOOOOOO SWEEEEEEET

to hear you, Bobby Lee.
I never knew how happy I could be
to hear your big, loud
buzzing noise in my ear.

BZZZZZ---BZZZZZ--BZZZZZ

Bobby Lee, how come you are
not afraid of the **DARK**?
You never get scared and scream in the night.
Bobby Lee answers, "Because, Sunny Me,
you always shine in the darkness."

11

Bobby Lee sings the song...

BZZZ...... ME TO SLEEP

"Bobby Lee and Sunny Me,
together we SLEEP happy and free.
Good night, good night you Sleepeee- Heads,
as angels come dancing 'round our beds.

The moon and Stars Shine a little Light,
through our bedroom window every night.
Sunny Me shine so bright,
there's no more fear of darkness so SLEEP TIGHT.

Say a prayer and turn out the light,
Bobby Lee will BZZZZ you to sleep every night
Ha Ha... a BZZZZ....ing Melody!"

Sunny Me, darkness is not
a big bad monster
that can jump out of the
closet and get you.
God created nighttime so we can sleep.
We need sleep to rest our bodies,
so when morning comes we
will be ready to run, work,
play, think, laugh, and sing.

God knew we would be afraid
when daylight ends;
that is why He created a
nightlight for us.
God placed the moon
and stars in the sky
so we could believe He is there.

Hee hee...Haaa...awwwe...
Sunny Me, under the stars,
sleeping at night...
underneath God's glorious nightlight.

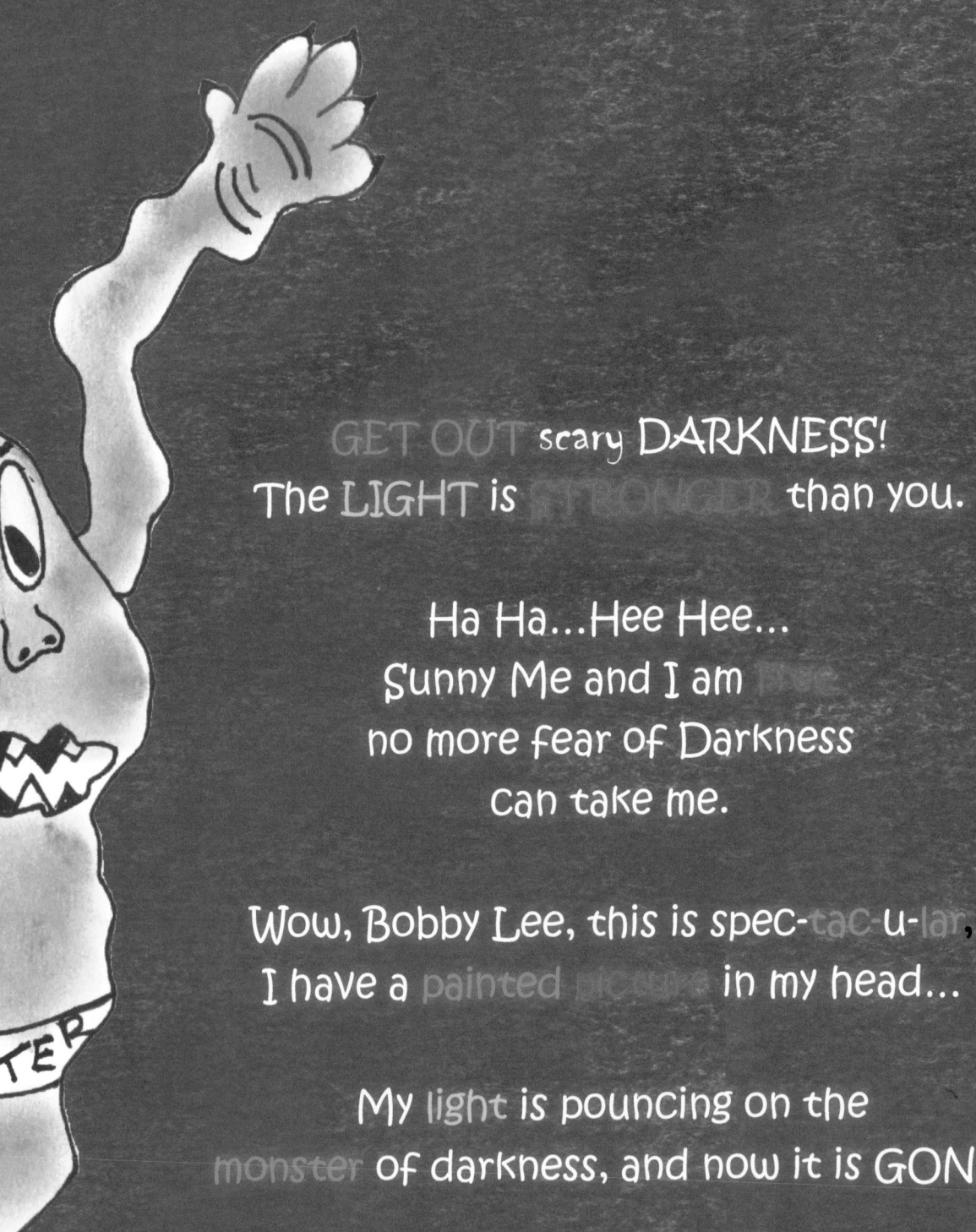

GET OUT scary DARKNESS!
The LIGHT is STRONGER than you.

Ha Ha...Hee Hee...
Sunny Me and I am free
no more fear of Darkness
can take me.

Wow, Bobby Lee, this is spec-tac-u-lar,
I have a painted picture in my head...

My light is pouncing on the
monster of darkness, and now it is GONE!

17

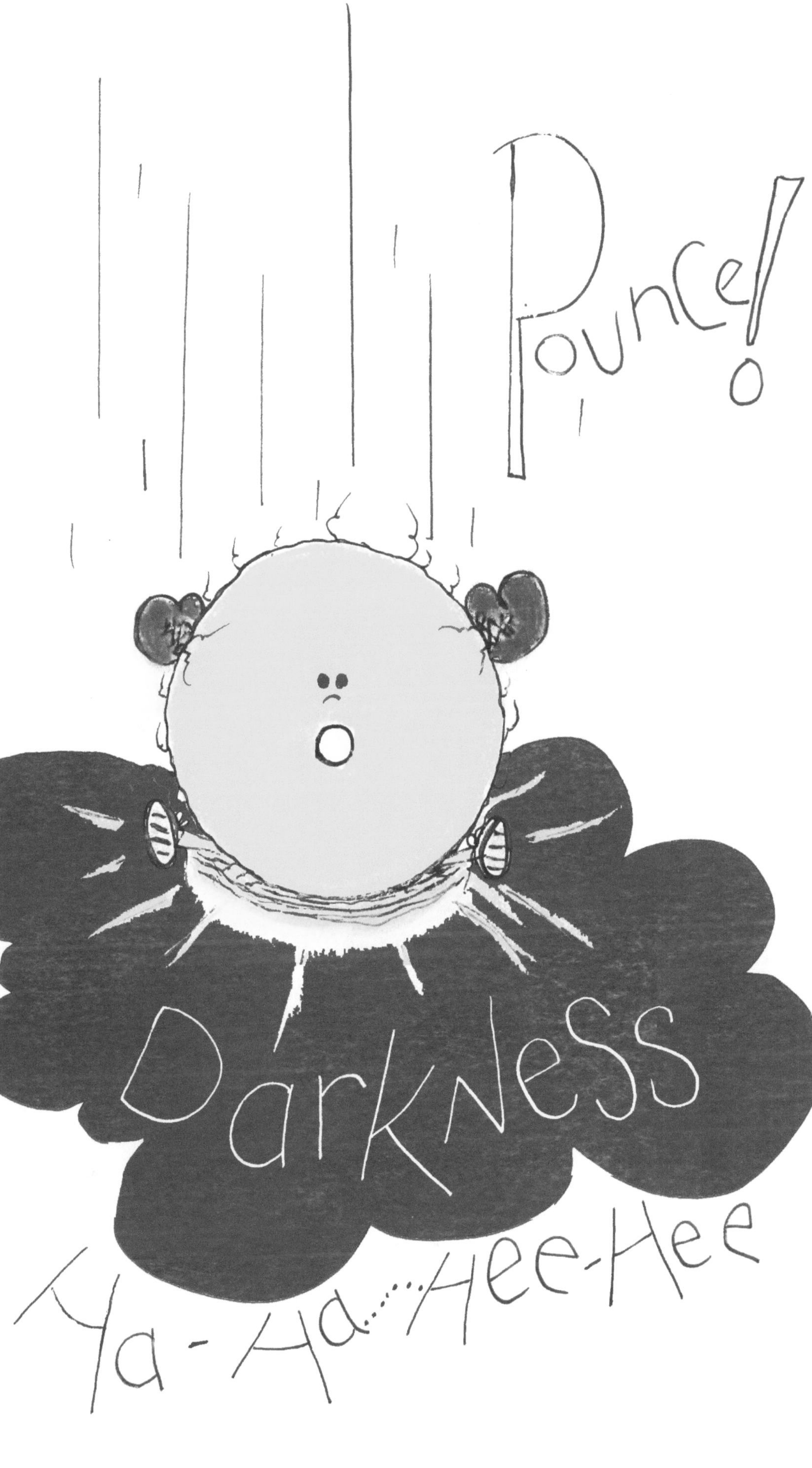
Pounce!
Darkness
Ha-Ha.....Hee-Hee

Hee...Hee...
Sunny Me

WHOO...HOO
ME and YOU

Smash-A-Roo

On the **DARK** too!

You are my best friend Bobby Lee,

I love you...

even though you make a lot of buzzing noise.
Ha-Ha.

Bobby Lee says, "What are friends for?
If I cannot be there when you need me the most,
then I guess I would not be a TRUE FRIEND at all."
"That's right, Bobby Lee, we have to stick together."

Stick TOGETHER like
HONEY and GLUE
ME and You!"

Bobby Lee says, "Sunny
Me, is a true friend
like a piece of bubble gum
that someone chewed and
spit on the ground...
and it sticks to your shoe... like glue?"

Suffering

Bzzz'n'z

Sticky-ness

Yep... "TRUE FRIENDS," describes me and you,
like gum on the shoe!

"Sticky one and sticky two,
here we go, just me and you...
me and you, me and you,
Slap-a-Roo

"the sticky two."

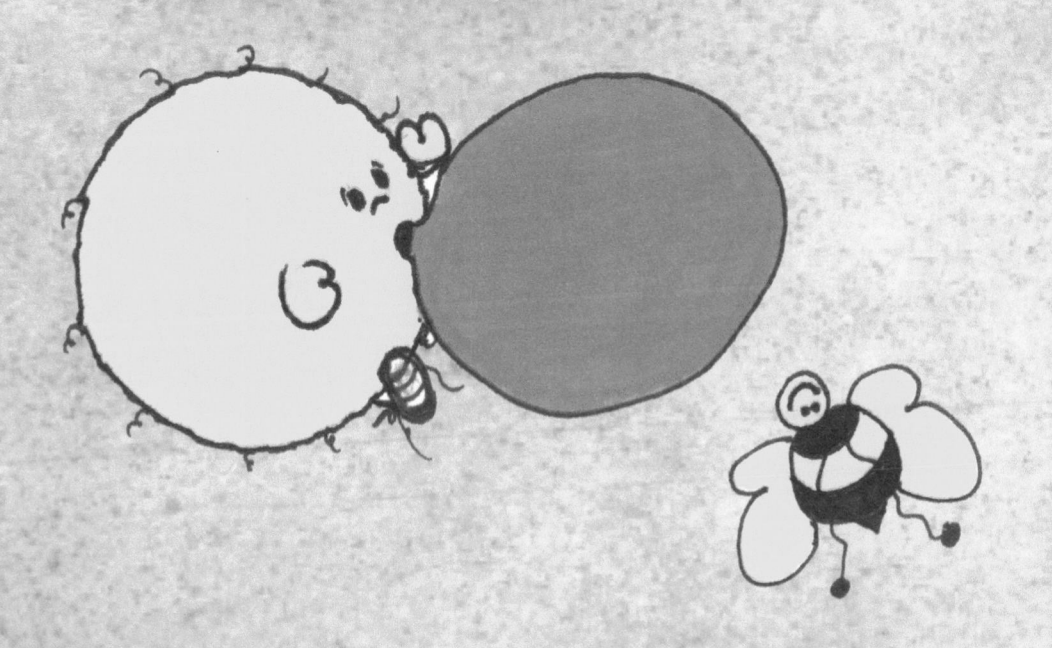

Sticky Me and sticky you
we will always...stick-a-roo.

I love making up little
tunes with words!
Hee hee...ha ha...
Sunny Me and Bobby Lee,
"the dynamic duo."

Bobby Lee says, "The dynamic yo-yo?"
"NO! That is not what I said,
we are a "duo"..."two"... "the dynamic duo!"

Let's make a tune Bobby Lee! OK?
I will START the tune...
"Ha ha...hee hee...blow me a bubble and slap a bee!"
Bobby Lee says, "flip -flop and zing-a-ling,
I can't make music so ding-a-ling-ling-ling!"

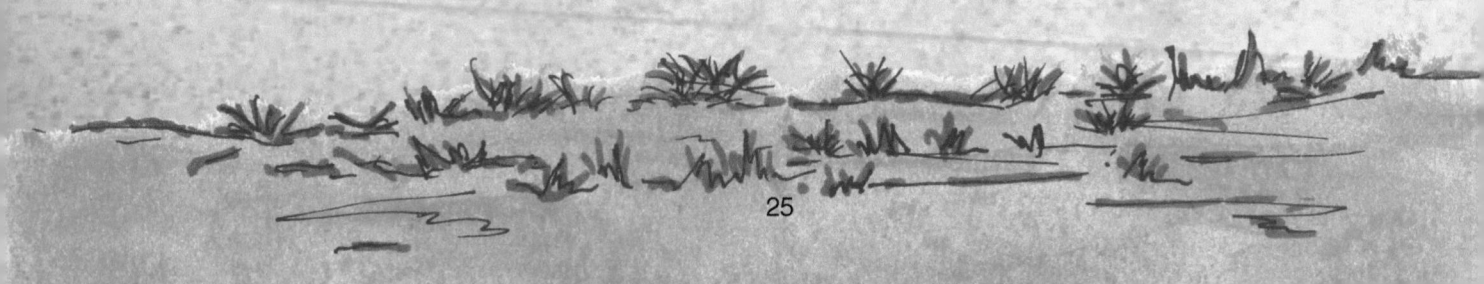

Bobby Lee, how did you
become so smart?

I want to be as smart as you so
I will not be afraid anymore.

Well, Sunny Me, have you seen the big oak tree in the middle of
O'Hagan Haven Park? It is the tree with a big open hole in the
trunk, holding a sign that says, "COUNSELOR."
Do you know the tree I am talking about Sunny Me?

Oh yes, Oh I know, I know,
the big oak tree in O'Hagan Haven Park.

Bobby Lee says, "Well, I was buzzing
around that tree one day and
out pops a big OWL's head, and he asked me
why I was buzzing around his tree.
I said, "I was looking for the counselor...
I heard that there was a counselor named 'CHieKO' here."
Then I said to the owl, "My friend, Sunny Me is
AFRAID of the DARK, and I want to help him.
Can you help us Chieko, the owl?"

"What did he say? what did
he say?" asked Sunny Me.
Chieko said, "Step into my office...
I mean, step into my yard of wisdom
and let me counsel you
a bit, Bobby Lee."

Bobby Lee says, "While waiting
patiently for the big answer
POW! Here it comes..."

Chieko says, "Sunny Me does not have
to be afraid of the **DARK**
because he is a sunshine, and there
will always be light in him.
Sunny Me is a BIG bright light!"

SMELLY Smarteee-Pants...
"YOU are a GENIOUS CHIEKO"!

Bobby Lee says, "Why didn't I think of that?"

29

Wow, Bobby Lee, this is why he has the name,
"The wise old owl,"
and people like to go sit under his tree and talk to him.
Hey, maybe we can visit Chieko tomorrow after school.
I wonder what else he might have to say to us.

Bobby Lee buzzes, "You had better get ready for your
ears to be burning and your legs to
be shorter, Sunny Me...
because once Chieko starts counseling,
he will talk your legs off."

TALK...TALK...TALK...
Talk, talk, talk, and your legs are short now!

Hee Hee... "Talk your legs off!"
You are so funny Bobby Lee,
turn your buzzer off and take a rest.

The next day, Sunny Me and Bobby Lee
walk up to the big oak tree and yell,
"Chieko, can you come out?"
POP!

Out comes his head and he says,
"Well, you are back Bobby Lee,
how may I help you?"

Chieko, I am Sunny Me, Bobby Lee's best friend.
We stopped by to thank you for
helping us and explaining that
light is in me, and it has more power than darkness.
Maybe we can visit with you more often and learn
about other things too.

We want to be SMART like you!

"Smart, smart, me and you...
Sunny Me, Bobby Lee, and Chieko too.
Walking in the light
and the **DARK** is out of sight."

We hope this story has helped you overcome
fear of nighttime and darkness too.

May your heart be full of light,
and your bed be full of sweet dreams every night.
Let's sing a goodnight song together...

From Sunny Me to Sunny You,
let's sing our nighttime melody we two.

"Good night, good night,
and oh...sleep tight,
no more fear of darkness can keep us awake at night.

Thank you, God, for the night light You bring,
we close our eyes, and hear the moon and stars sing.

Good night, good night,
we have a light,
we will close our eyes and SLEEP—TIGHT!

Thank you, God, for your
protection and light...
Night...Night."

Sunny Me ®

Other Books by Deborah Rowe Johnson

The Lost Boy

Raining Blessings

God Created Everything...
God Created Me

Lost & Found

One of a Kind

From Sunny Me to Sunny You!
Color Me Red, Paint Me Blue, Sign Me Green!

Bye, Bye.

About the Author

Deborah R. Johnson was born in Joplin, Missouri, in 1965, an identical twin, and a family of five. She moved to Temple, Texas, at the age of twelve and has been a native Texan ever since. She is a graduate of Southwest Texas State University with a Bachelor of Science in exercise physiology / health and nutrition. She is married to Toby Johnson and has been a teacher and coach for twenty-five years. This experience has enlightened her to create a fun-loving happy character for children and adults to enjoy. The Lord has blessed her with  the gift of writing and painting, and her business is called God's Reflections, Inc. Janice Rowe, Deborah's mother, spoke this business and knowledge of writing and painting into existence. If Deborah did not know the Lord and believe in his promises, this would have been unbelievable and probably nonexistent venture. She is thankful to the Lord for wisdom, faith, and the direction to study the Word in courses of study with Billy Graham Evangelist Association. This study has given her the knowledge needed to reveal the importance of spreading the good news, hope, and love to people all around the world. It is Deborah's prayer that Sunny Me touches the lives of many and inspires a desire to spread light and read more of God's Reflections books, greeting cards, and journals in the future. We are all God's Reflections, and she hopes that this book is an inspiration of light to all nationalities.